Patchwork

Numbers

Written by Felicia Law
Illustrated by Paula Knight

Norwood House Press

Chicago, Illinois

DEAR CAREGIVER

The **Patchwork** series is a whimsical collection of books that integrate poetry to reinforce primary concepts among emergent readers. You might consider these modern-day nursery rhymes that are relevant for today's children. For example, rather than a Miss Muffet sitting on a tuffet, eating her curds and whey, your child will encounter a Grandma and Grandpa dancing a Samba, or a big sister who knows how to make rocks skim and the best places to swim.

Not only do the poetry and prose within the **Patchwork** books help children broaden their understanding of the concepts and recognize key words, the rhyming text helps them develop phonological awareness—an underlying skill necessary for success in transitioning from emergent to conventional readers.

 As you read the text, invite your child to help identify the words that rhyme, start and end with similar sounds, or find the words connected to the pictures. The pictures in these books feature illustrations resembling the technique of torn-paper collage. The artwork can inspire young artists to experiment with torn-paper to create images and write their own poetry.

Above all, the most important part of the reading experience is to have fun and enjoy it!

Sincerely,

Shannon Cannon

Shannon Cannon, Ph.D.
Literacy Consultant

Norwood House Press • P.O. Box 316598 • Chicago, Illinois 60631
For more information about Norwood House Press please visit our website at
www.norwoodhousepress.com or call 866-565-2900.

LIBRARY OF CONGRESS CATALOGING-IN-PUBLICATION DATA
Law, Felicia.
  Numbers / by Felicia Law ; illustrated by Paula Knight.
     pages cm. -- (Patchwork)
  Summary: Torn paper collages and simple, rhyming text portray children experiencing numbers, from one child who wants to play alone to ten faces in disguise. Includes a word list.
  ISBN 978-1-59953-710-8 (library edition : alk. paper) -- ISBN 978-1-60357-808-0 (ebook)
[1. Stories in rhyme. 2. Numbers, Natural--Fiction.] I. Knight, Paula, illustrator. II. Title.
  PZ8.3.L3544Num 2015
  [E]--dc23
                         2014047192

274N—062015
Manufactured in the United States of America in North Mankato, Minnesota.

On my own

Leave me alone
    I've thrown
    All my toys away

Leave me alone
    All on my own
    I don't want to play

3

Two in the kitchen

Pudding bowls and rolling pins
    wooden spoons
Little pastry cutters
    in the shape of moons
Plates and saucers and
    jugs and bowls
Little pastry cutters
    that cut out holes

Mix it all together
    Stir it now and then
With little pastry cutters
    We make gingerbread men

6

Three somersaults

Look, I'm bending over
Doubling up in two
I can see between my legs
    And I can see you!

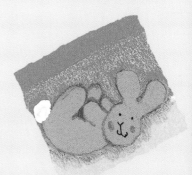

Faster and faster
Rocking to and fro
Watch me roly poly
    Over I go

Balancing on tiptoe
Pushing on my hands
Over I tumble
    Where will I land?

Four bits

This bit goes here

It's the one

That's the sun

It's yellow and hot

And it fits in
this spot

This bit goes there

Where?

There.

It's red

I think it's
the head

4

This bit goes here

It's green

And it fits

In between

The yellow and pink
I think

That bit is blue

That's why

I know

It's the sky

But where does
it go?

10

Five in a line

Sitting in the park
Watching the flowers
Passing the hours
Jo, Peter, Rose, Mel and me
Watching the world go by

No fuss
Just us
In the park

6 Skipping six

Hands up, hands down
We are skipping round
and round

Hands in, hands out
We are skipping all about

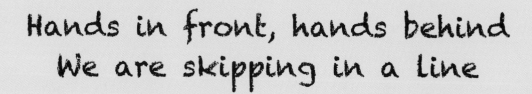

Hands in front, hands behind
We are skipping in a line

One two three four five six
Out I go and in you skip

(repeat)

13

7 Seven a-slide-y

Slippery slide-y
Take a ride-y
Seven a side-y
Down the slope

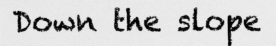

Slippery slide-y
Hands out wide-y
Sit beside me
Here we go!

15

Eight friends

My Mom said –

Which friends do you want
   to have at your party?

Do you want Jane and Zak
   and Jill and Marty?

Clive's a nice boy who
   always seems to care

You might enjoy the party if he was there

Cody's a jolly boy and likes to do tricks

And Simon is a funny kid –
   let's throw him in the mix ...

But darling – it's YOUR party

17

Nine in the pool

Come on, jump in the pool
   where it's cool
Let the water ripple
   between your toes
Duck below
   and hold your breath to three
Then blow
   like a whale
The water spouting from its nose

19

Ten faces

Princess, spaceman, leopard or clown

Flowers, spots and whiskers

Squiggles up and down

Face paint

Greasepaint

Nose and eyes

Nobody knows me

In my disguise!

21

This book includes these concept words:

- alone
- eight
- four
- bowl
- face
- gingerbread
- boy
- five
- hole

- hour
- one
- six

- jug
- park
- ten

- leave
- party
- three

- moon
- pastry
- toy

- nine
- plate
- two

- nose
- seven
- water

23